RAISING DEMONS

HELLFIRE SERIES NOVELLA

A Dark Paranormal Romance

CONTENTS

RAISING DEMONS	v
Blurb	vii
Inspiration	ix
Chapter 1	1
Chapter 2	11
Chapter 3	22
Chapter 4	29
Chapter 5	36
Chapter 6	42
Chapter 7	47
Chapter 8	50
Chapter 9	55
Chapter 10	65
Chapter 11	70
Chapter 12	79
Author's Note	89
About the Author	91

BLURB

As a demon who has become accustomed to the human way of life, Esmerelda will do whatever it takes to keep the food life she has built for herself. When she catches wind of a plan to raise an all-powerful demon that will ruin her good life topside, she has to take action. She only has one option; to stop them at all costs. On her quest to find out who is behind these nefarious plans, she meets Quinn, a devilishly handsome gargoyle who also hunts demons, just like her.

Can a demon and demon hunter really get along? Will Esmerelda and Quinn defy odds, even when her past comes to visit? Their world might get turned upside down and things might be over before they start.

INSPIRATION

The Hunchback of Notre Dame Fairytale

The Hunchback of Notre Dame, follows the story of Quasimodo. He is a bell-ringer of Notre Dame and hunchback who was abandoned by his mother and adopted by Archdeacon Claude Frollo. At a festival Archdeacon Claude Frollo is enthralled by the gypsy Esmerelda, who orders Quasimodo to kidnap her but Esmerelda is rescued by Captain Phoebus and Pierre Gringoire. He does so but is caught and flogged the following day for his crime and humiliated by the public. Feeling sorry for him, Esmerelda gives him water and a friendship formed.

Later on Esmerelda is arrested and charged for the

attempted murder of Phoebus, when it was actually Frollo who had attempted to kill him out of jealousy. She is sentenced to death by hanging by the King's men but is rescued by Quasimodo and taken to sanctuary.

Frollo informs Gringoire that her right to sanctuary is removed and Gringoire informs the leader of the gypsies who rallies the citizens of Paris to rescue her. She escapes, but Quasimodo thinks that the gypsies are trying to hurt her and drives them away. She is rescued by Frollo but he betrays her and watches while she is being hanged. Quasimodo isn't able to save Esmerelda and together they die.

All Rights Reserved
Copyright 2018 Amara Kent
No part of this book may be reproduced,
Distributed, transmitted in any form or by any
means, or stored in a database retrieval system
without the prior written permission of the
author. You much not circulate this book in any
format. Thank you for respecting the rights of the
author. This is a work of fiction. Any resemblance
of characters to actual persons, living or dead, is
purely coincidental.
Edited by TBR Editing and Eveis Kenevis. Cover
Designed by Brittany Van Lanen. All stock purchased.

CHAPTER ONE

I turn to the demon sitting on the chair in the middle of a trap I had created for him, spinning the dagger on my index finger and staring at him with a smirk plastered on my face. He stares back at me, a look of indifference on his face. He doesn't seem to care about being in the position he is in, or the fact that he is looking into the face of his torturer, the demon who has control of his life and could end it in an instant.

Does he even care why he is here I wonder. Is he aware that I will make him squeal like a little piggie for the information I need, that I'll rip the information from him. I need to know who is behind the plan, because the plan could destroy the very existence I've fought so hard to keep. A few days back, while minding my own business in a bar, I overheard from a couple of demons that someone was trying to raise an ancient and powerful evil, one I hadn't seen for a very long time.

I had managed to track down a demon who apparently knew some information which he had acquired from a mid-level demon. Demons are ranked, just like soldiers, a hierarchy that starts from the lowest rung on the ladder to the highest. Low-level demons are at the mercy of upper-level demons who are some the most powerful. I always look upon the hierarchy like chess pieces. Low-level demons are the pawns, considered disposable and just above that of humans. Mid-level demons are like your knights and bishops. They have a bit more power, more pull and are given tasks that are of some importance.

Upper-level demons are like your rooks. They not only perform the jobs that Lucifer hands down to them, they also have the power to do whatever they want that will please and benefit Lucifer in his quest for power. They deal with mid and low-level demons and help to cause hell on Earth by wreaking havoc.

There are only one set of demons that are above the upper-level ones, the top tier demons. This small group sits beside Lucifer. They are to Lucifer as Archangels are to God. They are his most trusted advisors and soldiers, his lieutenants, commanders and sergeants in a way. These demons are called in to create the most amount of destruction in the shortest amount of time, the ones who called upon The Four Horsemen in the very first apocalypse.

Others, thought they helped create The Apocalypse. They were deadly wrong. They didn't create The Apocalypse.

They *are* The Apocalypse.

Malphas, one of Lucifer's most trusted soldiers in the

fight against the forces of mankind and all things good, had risen through the ranks quickly, much to my discontent, and proved himself to be a force to be reckoned with.

He had created so much devastation and chaos on Earth that the angels had to step in. In the end it was the Archangel Michael who had defeated him, locking him in a fortress so impenetrable that no one was going to get in. More importantly, no one was going to get out.

Or so it seemed.

Someone, somewhere, has figured out how to release him - and now that

someone is planning on doing just that. They intend to bring him back up here to finish the job he had started all those centuries ago.

What I don't understand though is why him? There are plenty of other demons that could be chosen to bring on an apocalyptic event and wipe out the human race. So why him? What is so important about Malphas?

"So, tell me, who wants to free Malphas? Is it Leviathan? Azazel? Who?"

"I don't know." The demon seethes.

I let out an exasperated sigh.

Demons. Bunch of idiots.

"You know I can do this all day, for the rest of our lives in fact. I have nowhere to go, this is your decision. Tell me, or...." I walk up to him, take the dagger and slice his cheek, working diagonally from his right ear, down to the corner of his lips. He howls in pain as I grin menacingly at him.

He sneers at me and all I can do is let out a laugh at his futile attempts of intimidation.

"Why do you care about these pathetic humans anyway? You're a demon."

"I don't care about these humans. I care about this world. As you can see, I have built a pretty damn good life for myself, and *nothing*, I mean *nothing*, is going to ruin this for me. So, we can do this the hard way, or the easy way. And like you said, I'm a demon, so I know how to slowly torture a demon until they beg for death."

Silence.

I reach out to the wheelie tray next to me and pick up the syringe, dipping the needle into a bowl of holy water and filling it up to the brim. I don't bother to push out the air from the syringe, it doesn't matter to me whether it will affect him or not. I saunter over to him, grabbing his wrist and yanking it hard to straighten his arm.

I jab him with the needle and inject him with the holy water. He howls out in pain as the water makes its way through his body. To increase his suffering I stab him in the gut with the dagger just a little. Then, slicing into his flesh I create a deep gash in his body. Slowly, I remove the dagger, inch by painful inch, making sure that I'm causing the maximum amount of torment. I release him from the agony, and for a brief moment I give him some relief, a sense of finality, before I repeat the process over and over again.

When I've finished he lifts his head, eyes the colour of onyx boring into me.

"Who is behind the plan to bring Malphas back?" I question again.

"It won't matter, he will rise again, and when he does, I will take pleasure in torturing you for the rest of your miserable life!"

I let out a raucous laugh." You? Torture me? You don't seem the type to be able to torture puppies, let alone a demon of the Underworld a lot more powerful than you."

"If I don't, then he will... When he's released."

He isn't entirely wrong there. If Malphas is released and finds me, he will revel in the chance to give me my comeuppance. He will literally scour the globe to come find me and give me what he thinks I deserve.

"Don't you worry about me demonling, I'm a big girl. I can take care of myself."

Facing my tray of torture instruments, I run my fingers over them, contemplating which one to use next, passing over four and stopping at a tool I had yet to use. There aren't many out there that can be used to torture or kill a demon, apart from the usual holy water, runes and a dagger that literally poisons and kills the demon from inside it's vessel.

I actually have very little need for tools of torture. I no longer worry myself about the dealings of demons and keep out of their business. They had become somewhat like a security blanket for me though, as I have had run ins with the odd demon here and there. I don't need them, but I'd hate to not have them.

"Why do you have to torture all the time Dee? You can easily *just get the information from him by seeing into his mind."* My vessel, Vee asks. I can actually picture her pouting.

"This is much more fun though Vee. If you don't like it, go back to your little corner like you always do."

I feel her sulking. She hesitates, but leaves me in peace anyway. My vessel, Esmerelda, is a gypsy. Actually, she's Gitano, who are basically Romani, but Spanish. I've been advised by Esmerelda that gypsy is incredibly derogatory and should never be used. When I first came across her, she was living in an abusive relationship with her dick of a husband. He was all kinds of asshole, beating her, cheating on her, controlling their financials and degrading her. I can't stand women being treated in such a way. So, when she was praying to the all mighty, the biggest of all douches and the Le King Twatbag, I intercepted her call and came to her rescue instead.

I had grown tired of my vessel and it was about time that I upgraded to a new model. It's a practice I keep to stop Lucifer from hunting me. There is no way I wanted to show up on his radar, so when my vessel had served their time I traded them in for a new model and moved on. Just like buying a car. It's a lonely life, sure, but I have little room for friends, cause that's when shit sneaks up on you and back-hands you in the face. The more people that know you, the easier you are to track.

I had taken it upon myself to perform my civic duty and get rid of her husband. She was eternally grateful and asked what I wanted in return. I was ecstatic, here was this woman, asking me what *I* wanted! So I told her that I could use a new body and surprisingly she agreed to house me. Stupid? Probably, but for the most part we have a very good working relationship with each other. On the odd occasion I would slip into demon mode, like right now, I could feel her shouting at me to stop doing what I'm doing. I usually tell her to go away and leave me alone. Sometimes she puts up a fight but other times, like now, she would just sulk and go away into the background.

She has actually built a little home in my... her... mind. She is literally a passenger of her own body. I am the driver, taking lead and making her body do as I wish. When she first spoke to me after I possessed her she called me demon. She refused to call me Esmerelda because she knew the difference, unlike the people around us. In return, I called her vessel. She hated the name, so obviously I continued. Now we just call each other Dee and Vee.

I picked up the tool, which I call Maggie. It was aptly named after a girl I knew who liked to fuck people. A lot. This weird looking instrument has two forks that branch off from the handle. Attached to the forks are circular iron meshes with a pentagram surrounded by runes engraved on both sides. On the frame holding the mesh are hooklike teeth which when plunged into skin embed themselves into the flesh.

I acquired this magnificent tool when I came across a hunter who had been killed by a demon. The demon, being of a one-track mind, missed the most valuable item. I'm not complaining, it was a win for me.

What makes it so insanely perfect is its ability to inflict a constant stream of pain. This comes from the pentagram and runes and, if you are so inclined, you can twist it and allow the little hooks to do their job. It is truly a magnificent instrument of torture.

Without giving him the chance to figure out what I'm doing, I rip open his shirt and jam Maggie into his chest. A sound emanates from him like the possessed girl from the Exorcist.

I pick up the pistol I had attained over a decade ago. It is loaded with bullets that are not only coated with holy water, but filled with it. Once the bullets make themselves at home in the body they dissolve, releasing a slow stream of holy water.

The hunter who had made it was a genius.

I fire a couple of rounds into his stomach. His screaming becomes even louder. I can't help the wide devilish smile from forming on my face, satisfied with the pain I'm inflicting on him.

"Now, before I proceed, will you tell me who is behind all this?" I ask in a sickly sweet manner.

He's going to break soon, I can tell by the way beads of sweat that are forming on his forehead, slithering down his face like a snake.

All it's going to take is a little extra convincing for him to squeal like a little piggie. I inject holy water all over his face, one shot straight after the other. In the end, his face looks like he's received six degree burns. Quite a horrendous sight. If I wasn't a demon, I would have upchucked from the look of him.

"I told you, I don't know who is behind it!"

"Bullshit! As if you don't know!" I'm getting tired of this. I had been torturing him for hours and still nothing. "One more time you asswipe! Tell me who the *fuck* is behind this!"

I grab the hilt of Maggie and twist it whilst pushing it in further.

"Okay, okay!" His breath comes out wheezy like a smoker who has been going at it for 10 years. "I don't know who is behind it, but I do know that they are looking for the Book of the Dead which is located at the Church of Notre Dame in Washington DC, America."

"You mean Paris?" Not trying to stop the condescension flowing out with my words.

"No, you need to go to the one in America."

"Right." I say, extending the word.

I eye him, squinting, taking it in all in and deciding whether or not he is telling me the truth.

He is.

"I believe you."

A relieved sigh escapes his lips. "Good, can you let me go?"

"Hmmmm. . . . Okay!" I flick my hand out at him as if I'm flicking water off my hand and his whole body explodes before me.

I pick up the hand towel from the railing on the tray and wipe away the blood and guts. I usually don't dispose of demons this way, it's too messy and smells *really* bad. I don't know whether it's because I have lived amongst the humans for most of my life or whether it's always smelt like this bad, but the gut wrenching, vomit inducing odour of burning flesh is not something I found appetising.

It's a smell that stinks up the room for days, seeping into all the little crevices. It clings to your clothes, and your skin if you are exposed to it for too long. And the bones! Don't get me started on the bones. I once found bones of a demon I had killed a year after I had done it when I was living in the Underworld.

CHAPTER TWO

Not wanting to touch the remnants of the demon, I snap my fingers and allow my powers to do the job for me. Sometimes it's great being a demon. I know, totally lazy, but I *hate* cleaning. I walk out of my little den of torture and head up the stairs and to my bathroom which is connected to my bedroom. I am in desperate need of a shower, as I smell like sweaty ball sack and need to scrub every inch of my body clean. I walk into the bathroom, strip off, fiddle with the taps until the water is a perfect temperature and step in.

There aren't many things in the human world that I love, even with living here for nearly a century. I've never understood how humans could be into half the shit they are into. Though there is one thing that they got right, and that is the ability to live in luxury. Living in the deep and dingy depths of the Underworld my room was not as bad as others, but it was nothing like what I have now. Now I'm living in luxury in a mini mansion. It is an older style Spanish home on the outskirts of Sarria-Sant Gervasi in Barcelona, Spain. The beautiful white stone home with it's red rooftop is tucked away on an acreage. It's peaceful and relaxing and I can go about my day without anybody bothering me.

I finish scrubbing myself raw and, satisfied that I smell clean and decent, towel myself off and walk to my cupboard. I had acquired quite a wardrobe. I'm very materialistic, which surprises me, but I'm in a hot ass vessel and she needs to be shown off. After being repressed for so long, Esmerelda needed some time to let loose and get all loosey goosey. At first she wasn't a fan of my very, ummm, promiscuous lifestyle, but eventually she just dealt with it and took a backseat whenever I would go hard on some guy. Yes, as much as I hate humans, the men are *very* useful.

I fish out a pair of navy blue shorts then a black tank top and put them on along with a pair of socks and my black combat boots. Grabbing my phone from the bed I look at the time. It's 3:00am here in Spain, which means that it's roughly 10:00 pm in America. This is a good time to go to the church, there shouldn't be anyone there.

I look up the Church of Notre Dame in Washington DC on my phone. It has some information on it, but all I need is a picture of the inside to be able to teleport myself to it. I go to the photo gallery and find enough photos of the exterior and interior, and I teleport myself into the little entrance of the church. I expect to be greeted by the sound of silence, but instead, I'm greeted by the sounds of a struggle. Opening the door to the church slightly, I peer in and what I see actually stuns me.

"Woah, who's that?" Vee asks.

"You're seeing the same thing I am, at the same time I am. How the hell am I supposed to know?" I snap at her.

I feel like I'm watching a movie and have a sudden urge to cook up some popcorn, sit in one of the pews and watch the scene that's unfolding before me. A man is fighting off three demons and doing a rather good job of it. He is definitely no stranger to fighting them as he expertly kills them one at a time. Just as he is about to kill the third, he is suddenly thrown across to the side stone wall and pinned there. I look to the demon responsible for this. He is in a relaxed stance, hand held up like he is pushing something and walking, no, stalking towards the man.

I'm so enthralled that I almost miss the demon that is slinking in the shadows, his movements lithe as he heads my way. If it hadn't been for the moonlight catching the brass on the book he's carrying, I wouldn't have even seen him.

"Are you going to get him?" Vee asks quietly.

"No, I can't just go in and wipe the demon out. I have to do this with as little hassle as I can and as quietly as I can. I don't want the other demon to know that I'm here."

"Do you think that's the Book of the Dead?"

"Demons in a church and one is carrying a thick book, sneaking away? I have no doubt."

I wait in my spot, not wanting to give my position away so I can take out the demon swiftly and silently, without alarming the other demon in the room who is still preoccupied with his little pet. I wait with bated breath as he comes closer and closer.

Come on.

He is close to the last row of pews when my attention is torn away from my demon target. I hear the distinct sound of a person being choked to death. The gurgling and rasping sound of someone trying to inhale against a force that is pushing down on their windpipe. I ignore the sound, he can take care of himself and if not, it is not my problem. My job is to get the Book of the Dead and destroy it so it can't be used to raise Malphas.

"You have to help him!" Vee shouts, creating an annoying ringing in my head.

"No, I don't. He'll be fine."

"HELP HIM!" She screeches.

Ouch! Bitch, that hurt my head.

"Fine!"

Just before the demon can reach me, I burst through the church doors and throw the demon that pinned the guy across to the back of the church with my powers. His body hits it with the force of a wrecking ball at full swing. I teleport right in front of the demon holding the book in his vice like grip and punch him. This unfortunately doesn't have the effect that I needed, and I immediately regret not doing something more when he throws me across the church. I land right on the back of the pews, a crack resounding off the walls.

Ugh, you fucking cocksucker.

I get on my hands and knees, waiting for the sharp pain

to dissipate before I stand up and brush myself off. The demon goes to attack me with a kick but I'm ready for him. I grab his leg and snap it, the sound of bone breaking meeting my ears. He screams out in pain as he drops to the floor, the book sliding across and stopping between two pews. I take this opportunity to make a grab for the book but before I can run to get it I'm kicked in the back of my legs. Still falling to my knees, he whacks me in the back of my head and I land flat on my face.

I'm jerked from my resting place on the floor and brought up to above his height by my neck, my feet flailing around below me. My entire body is jerking back and forth so much that I look like I am either having a fit in the air or fucking a ghost. Like a fish out of water.

Damn he's strong.

I manage to look down and see that his broken leg is resting on the ground, putting all his weight on his good leg, looking quite like a lame horse.

With all the power I can muster, I shoot him across the room and fall to the ground, grasping at my neck and rubbing the sore spot while my breathing returns to its regular pace. I look up to see the demon stalking towards me. Well, stalk limping towards me? This guy must be made of rock or hocked up on energy drinks or something because nothing is bringing him down. Great, I'm dealing with the man of steel.

I decide to bring out the big guns to end this fight so I can grab the book. I freeze him in place, closing the distance between us and placing my hands on either side of his head.

Using my powers, I start to drain the life away from him. I watch as the colour slowly drains from his face. His skin turns a sickly grey and blood starts trickling from his ears. He must have put this vessel through hell and killed it.

Most demons did, they didn't like the human fighting against them. Killing them kept the voices away.

I usually followed the same practice, but I had saved Vee from certain death at the hands of her husband. I wasn't going to go and kill her after saving her life.

Maybe I'm becoming more human.

A wide grin forms on my face, I can't help feeling extremely satisfied at my kill. I walk over to where I see the Book of the Dead and pick it up. Taking a look over at the demon and the man going at it, I'm shocked when I see wings spanning behind the man as he lifts himself off the ground. A tail trails behind him, the end of it coming to a point like an arrow.

Gargoyle.

The gargoyle flies straight at the demon, knocking him into the ground with a loud thud. Whomever this gargoyle is, he is mesmerising to watch. He moves with such fluidity that he's more like water than an actual gargoyle which is made of stone and known to be quite stiff.

I internally giggle from my sad little joke.

It's a beautiful dance of swinging fists and flying feet, his elegant movements so graceful. For the majority of the fight the gargoyle has been the one in front, he has had the upper hand. And then somehow, in the blink of an eye, the demon has him pinned against the wall again. It doesn't matter how strong the gargoyle is or that he can fly, he is no match for the demon. He strides towards the gargoyle, claws extended, his movements lithe and calculating. Animalistic, like a panther stalking his prey.

He walks up to the man and just as he moves his arm back to take a swing at him, I intercept. Using my own powers, I throw him across the church. The hold that had pinned the gargoyle against the wall breaks and he falls to the ground. The demon instantly jumps back up and uses his powers on me. Well tries to, anyway. I smirk as he attempts to take me down, throwing shot after shot of energy at me.

I freeze him in place and watch him try to move, but he can't move an inch. The tension is evident on his face as beads of sweat start dripping down.

"Now, I'm going to unfreeze you so we can talk. Try anything and you will regret it." I explain.

I release him from my power. He goes to throw me across the room but I stop him short and pin him to the floor where he can't move and put up an invisible wall so if he uses his powers, it will be on himself. I walk over to the gargoyle, who is now standing, watching us.

"Are you okay?"

"Yes." he says gruffly, the deep and rich tone of his voice music to my ears, hitting me in all the wrong places. Well right places, but wrong for me.

"Do you need help? You took quite a beating."

He grunts as he pushes passed me, making his way to the demon and standing in front of him.

"Wow, dick much?" I mumble.

I hear Vee groan.

He swings his head around so fast it looks like it's going to snap off. "What did you say?!" he growls.

I hate it when people play this stupid little game, like they have no idea what you said. They know very well, it's so irritating.

"You heard me, I said. *Wow. Dick. Much,*" I say to him in a condescending tone. "I just asked a fucking question and instead of answering me you grunt at me like a Neanderthal and push passed me. Oh, and by the way, you're *welcome!* It was no problem saving your life."

"I had the situation under control." He says.

"Oh yeah, you were in the winning position! If this was a paid fight, I would have totally bet against the demon." I respond sarcastically.

All I receive is a low, grumbling growl.

Oh for shit's sake, are you serious?

"Is that deep throated growl supposed to intimidate me? Scare me? Have me shaking my boots?"

Another growl.

Does this gargoyle have any other threat at his disposal other than growling like a dog? He is seriously in need of a 101 lesson in intimidation.

"Okay enough of this, what are you wanting with the demon, and who are you?" I demand.

"That's none of your concern, *demon*." he spits out, hate and disgust evident when he says the word demon.

"Well it is, otherwise I wouldn't be standing here… Instead, I would be in Aruba, soaking up the sun and getting even browner than I already am. So, out with it. Who are you?"

Ignoring me, he turns his attention to the demon in front of him. "What are you doing here?"

"Fuck off!" *Well that went as well as expected.*

He takes a step forward, so close to the demon that they could have made out. He straightens up, trying to appear much taller. He isn't. It's a very futile attempt at intimidation. Shit, this guy needs help.

"I won't ask again. Tell me, what you are doing here." Again, the low timbre of his voice hit me in all the right places. Just at the wrong time. Is it normal for someone to feel incredibly turned on when in a heated situation like the one I'm in?

"No, no it isn't. But he is hot though. Incredibly. Are you sure he's a gargoyle? Aren't they usually ummm... ugly?" Vee asks.

"I'm definitely sure, but I get what you mean. Gargoyles are usually ugly, stumpy little stone things. Not the dirty blonde Adonis standing before us."

"You're a fucking idiot if you think I'm going to tell you anything, gargoyle." I turn my attention back to the demon and the gargoyle.

"I was hoping you would say that." The menacing grin and voice dripping of death made it clear of his intention to torture it out of him if he didn't comply.

His tail snakes up the demon's body, coiling itself around him slowly as it works its way up. I then watch the tip of the tail which is made of metal, and not skin and muscle like the rest of it. Before I know it, the arrow tip of the gargoyle's tail pierces straight through the ear and out the other side, crimson liquid flowing out of his ears. The demon jolts in shock, shaking from the intruder inside his skull.

"Are you willing to talk now?" He asks almost nonchalantly.

The demon twitches and nods. Quickly, the gargoyle removes his tail from inside the demon's head.

Crumbling into a heap on the floor, the demon hunches over. He spits out blood and starts laughing, sounding much like a mad scientist.

"You can do whatever you want to me, I will never tell you."

"He's right you know?" I interject. "You can do whatever the hell you want to do to him, he's never going to tell you. Well, not with your tactics."

The gargoyle moves so quickly in front of me that I take a step back to distance myself.

"And what would you know?"

"Hellooooo! Demon! For shit's sake, where did you get your lack of knowledge on demons from? A school for bunnies?" I go to shove him out of the way but the guy is a brick house.

Damn!

"Why don't you let me demonstrate my knowledge of demons on you then, Demon." he sneers.

"The little that you know would do nothing to me. Now step aside, while I *actually* get the information out of this guy."

He steps in front of me as I try to get to the demon, blocking me with his wings. I groan.

You've got to be kidding me.

While he is so concerned with my presence at the church, he's failed to notice the demon that was once crouched on the floor has moved and is making his way towards the church door.

"Look, this isn't the time to be bickering like an old married couple." I turn and freeze the demon . . . again.

CHAPTER THREE

I walk over and stand in front of the demon and smile. I wave my hand in front of his face, releasing the freeze from his head only.

"Hiiii, now, here's how things are going to go. You will tell me, one way or another, who is behind the plans to raise Malphas—"

"Malphas?" Gargoyle asks.

I roll my eyes. "Yes, Malphas. Now shut up and let me do my thing." I face the demon and flash him a smile. "Now, as I was saying. Before I was *rudely* interrupted. Sorry about that, gargoyles right?" I chuckle, which earns yet another growl from the gargoyle behind me. "You *will* tell me one way or another who is behind the plan to raise Malphas. I already know that it involves one of the few gates to the Underworld, and the Book of the Dead…

"The Book of the Dead." I whip around to face the gargoyle.

"What are you a fucking parrot! Shut. The hell. Up!" I bark at him. He goes to speak and I hold up my finger. "No! One more word out of you and I will sew your mouth shut you hear me?" No protest. "Good."

I turn my attention back to the demon. "So, what is it going to be? You can either give up the information now, or I literally force it out of you. The ball is in your court." My jovial tone doesn't seem to sit well with the demon.

"I'm not telling you anything she-devil, so you can shove it up your ass!"

Why do demons never go for the easy option? It always ends badly for them. I always end up killing their demonic selves.

I shrug.

I place my hands on either side of his head and focus on seeing into his mind. Instantly images flash before my eyes. I see what he has seen and experienced. I'm hoping for and searching for something that can tell me who is behind the whole thing, but nothing. All I can see is him going about his pathetic and boring life. I'm just about to give up when an image of him meeting with a demon I recognise comes into view. He is talking to Kane, a mid-level demon who thinks he's much more powerful and stronger than he actually is, about the plans to release Malphas. They are discussing how they need to find the Book of the Dead and the keys in order to release Malphas from his cage.

I remove my hands, stopping the images that are playing like a film, after the discussion between the two demons.

"I'd say thank you for the information, but you really didn't give it me of your own free will. Soooo..."

"How did you do that? Only upper-level demons have the power to see into another being's mind." The shocked expression on the demon's face brings a sense of satisfaction to me.

I think about how I manage to be in the presence of two stupid, stupid beings. What were the odds that not only would I run into Tweedle Dee, but also Tweedle Dum? "You just answered your own question there Einstein. Geeze, are you naturally this dumb or have you had one too many hits to the head?"

"Tell me who you are!" He demands.

"Ahhh, no."

"Tell me or I'll—"

"Or you'll what? May I remind you that you are in the presence of an upper-level demon. One that can kill you with the snap of her fingers." I snap my fingers to demonstrate just how easy it could be. "Actually, that gives me a brilliant idea!"

"Don't, stop!" Gargoyle shouts behind me.

I snap my fingers and the demon drops to the floor.

He is dead.

I have killed him.

"What the fuck was that for?!" he exclaims

I feign cluelessness. "Why, whatever do you mean?" I spin around to face him.

"Why did you kill the demon?"

"Because he was useless, he was getting on my nerves and the information he gave, I already knew."

"And what if I had questions?"

"He honestly wasn't going to tell you anything else. I got everything I needed from being inside his tiny head, which was nothing. You know, we could always team up? You look like you could be useful to me..." I look him up and down. "Somehow. Maybe as a lackey or something."

"No—" he says shortly. "Just tell me what you *fucking* saw."

I let out an exasperated sigh. "He was having a meeting with another demon, Kane, real slime ball and a massive prick. I still don't know who is planning on raising Malphas, but I do know that in order to do so, the demon will need to know the locations to one of the main gates to the Underworld, this book." I pat the book that's sitting under my arm. "And three keys, whatever that means."

"Okay, now hand the book over." He holds out a beckoning hand.

I stare at his outstretched hand and then at him and scoff. "Are you stupid?"

"Huh?"

"Are you stupid?" I repeat.

"What does that—"

I interrupt impatiently. "Because only a stupid person would think that I'd hand over this book, the Book of the Dead, the book that is said to contain the spell needed to raise a demon of Malphas' strength and power to the surface. I'm going to burn it, so it can never be used."

"You can't do that." His tone a mix of shock and anger.

"Oh I can't, can't I? Says who? You? HA!"

"There are other spells in there that may be worthwhile one day, there is a reason why it's been kept intact for all these years. Give it to me and I'll protect it."

I don't try and hold back the laughter that forces its way out of my mouth. I can't believe this guy. "Oh shit man, there are not enough ways to say no to you. I'm going to burn this thing and there is nothing that you can say or do to stop me."

He grabs my shoulder and squeezes hard.

Going to play that game huh?

I immediately throw him against the wall on the other side of the church and teleport over to him, crouching down to where he is crumpled on the floor. "You know, even though you have been a Grade A dick to me this whole time, my offer still stands. I will no doubt need help with this whole, stopping a potential apocalypse from occurring. Are you in or out?"

"Fuck off!" He sneers

I shrug. "Suit yourself!"

With that, I teleport out of there and back to my home in Barcelona. Standing in my room I toss the book on the bed, flopping down next to it and letting out a sigh. It has been a long day, and I'm exhausted. Demons don't usually get exhausted, we have enough power to sustain us for weeks. We can even go without sleep for days on end and be totally fine. Between getting my ass somewhat kicked and having to deal with Mr Broody McDicknuts back at the church, I'm spent and in some serious need of a good massage by a hot Spanish man.

I close my eyes as I picture getting covered in massage oil, a smoking hot masseuse moving his skilled hands over the contours of my body, up my legs, before settling on the sweet spot between my thighs. I shake myself out of my erotic thoughts when I notice my hand has dipped beneath my shorts and panties. Pulling my hand out I spring up to a sitting position.

"Need a cold shower?" Vee giggles.

"Oh quiet you!" Her loud laughter fills my head.

Ignoring her, I grab the book and start flipping through it.

I need to find the specific spell that they were looking for, if it exists in this book. Unfortunately, with a book titled *Book of the Dead* there are many spells that can be used to conjure up such a demon. The sound of my stomach grumbling tells me that I'm hungry, making me realise that I hadn't actually eaten for weeks.

I get up and walk to the kitchen, taking the book with me. I'll whip myself up some food and read through it while I eat. I place the book on my dining table and walk to the fridge. Peering in I realise I haven't done any grocery shopping in a while. It is a good thing that I have some ready-made meals in the freezer. Grabbing myself a creamy chicken pesto pasta, I open the throw away container and hold my dinner in my hands, allowing heat to radiate from them to defrost and heat up my meal. When it's hot enough, I open the lid, grab a fork from a drawer and sit down at the table where I had placed the book.

I am halfway through the book when I find the spell that could be used to raise Malphas. I feel rather triumphant and incredibly pleased with myself. Why? It is a boring book to read, I'm surprised that I lasted this long without falling into a deep sleep. I have no purpose for most of the spells in it. There is no interest there anymore. If I was the old me, I would be grabbing the ingredients to perform them as quickly as possible. I am just about to read through the rest of the spell when I'm dragged out of my perfect little haven and standing back in the church again.

CHAPTER FOUR

"You've got to be kidding me!" I'm absolutely livid. I've been summoned, and not just by anybody, but by the asshat gargoyle. I stand there and glare at him. "What the hell do you want?!"

"Well hello to you too." He smirks.

"What the hell do you want?" I repeat.

"I want the book and seeing as though you won't give it up, and I have no idea what is really going on around here, I thought that, well, I thought that we could work together," he says, mumbling the last bit.

"He wants to work with you now? I wonder what made him change his mind." Vee muses.

"Mmmhmm. . . . I'm thinking exactly the same thing."

I can't believe he wants to work with me now. Does he really think that I'm going to just say 'Okay! Let's do this!'

"And what makes you think I want to work with you? As I recall, you knocked me back not once, but twice when I offered so nicely for us to partner up. So before I tell you to go fuck yourself, why do you want to work with me, why the change of heart?"

"Because since you left, I've had more demons crash the place, looking for the book. A book that is no longer here because it's with you. Where is the book?"

"Hmmm, interesting. Well, I'm sorry, but no. . .Oh, and go fuck yourself."

"Where is the book?" he barks at me.

"I was reading it back at my place, and then my ass was summoned back here. By you." I go to leave, but I'm stopped short by the gargoyle.

"You are in a trap, so there is no use trying to teleport out of here this time. You need my help, otherwise you wouldn't have asked me to begin with, so why are *you* changing *your* mind this time?"

"He's got a point there."

I mentally growl at Vee.

I look down and sure enough, there, clear as day, are the placement of five crystals in the shape of a pentagram with runes painted on the inside. This gargoyle has done his research since our first encounter. I'll give him a C for effort.

"Look, you don't trust me and I get that. I'm a demon, we aren't to be trusted. But I really don't want to try and convince you that I am not trying to fuck you over and that I will never hurt you, like we're in a relationship and you're some needy chick. So *that's* why I retract my previous offers. I don't want to have to constantly reassure you."

He sighs and says reluctantly, "Look, I can't watch the

church the whole time and during the day I revert back to being a stone gargoyle sitting on top of the church. I need another set of eyes and a body that is free to walk around in the day to help me."

"Wow, are you actually admitting to needing me gargoyle?" I ask, relishing the moment.

He grimaces, his jaw clenching tightly as he nods.

Oh this is sweet.

"I wanna hear you say it. Tell me that you want me, and need me... Desperately" I say seductively.

He just sits there, glaring at me.

I hold up my hands in a placating gesture. "Okay, okay, fine. I'll work with you."

I step out of the trap that he had placed and walk over to him.

I bask in the moment of seeing the shocked expression on his face, and shrug. "What? You really didn't think a trap like that could contain me? Oh please, I'm much more powerful than those weak little traps. I guess, now that we are working together, I will need to be here in America, which means I need a place to stay. Where do you live?"

"You aren't staying with me. I may have agreed to work with you on this because you are useful, but you aren't staying with me."

"Fine, well I'll need a hotel then. I'm Esmerelda by the way. What's your name?"

"Quinn."

"Quinn? Isn't that a girl's name?" I laugh

"It's a unisex name!" he bites out through clenched teeth, sounding more like he's constipated than pissed off.

"Okay, okay! Whatever you say." I lift my hands up in an act of surrender.

"Wow, he's sensitive," Vee says.

"It's so a girl's name right Vee?"

"Right."

"So, where are the good places to stay around here?"

"You can stay at the Washington Hotel uptown."

"Cool." I pull out my phone and search on Google for the hotel, finding a map of the place. "Let's get going."

"I'm not going with you," he says flatly.

"I don't know about you, but I actually like this world and hope to live in it for as long as possible, which means that we need to act on this ASAP."

I take his hands in mine, I feel him pull away but I hold my grip. Without saying a word, I teleport us straight to the outside of the hotel. We show up behind a tree so that we won't be seen. I am so used to teleporting that I forgot what it's like the first time. I smile as he keels over, resting his hands on the tree, his face sheet white, looking like he's going to vomit.

"You okay there Quinnie boy?"

"Don't. Call. Me. Th…" Retching sounds meet my ears as I watch him throw up the contents of his stomach.

"You'll be fine. Give it a few minutes and you'll be okay. The first time is always a little painful." I say giving him a wink.

A few minutes later he is good to go and all the colour

that had previously left his body like it was repulsed by him has returned.

I conjure up two sets of luggage, garnering an odd look from Quinn. "It's about perception Quinnie boy. If we go in there and book out a hotel room with no luggage, you are going to look like a man who has just paid a prostitute for a root."

We walk into the grand lobby of the hotel, marble flooring stretches out as far as the eye can see. It is all white with only a splatter of colour here and there, browns and maroons mostly. To the left is a little sitting area where people can sit and chat. A set of steps lead to the front reception area which we make our way to, shoes clicking along as we walk, echoing thrughout the expansive hotel lobby. We are pretty much the only ones there, allowing us the luxury of walking straight up to the reception desk without having to wait in line.

"Hi, welcome to the Washington Hotel, are you checking in?"

"Yes, we are." I answer sweetly

"Okay, wonderful. Now what kind of room are you looking to book with us?"

"A suite if you have one available."

"Fantastic! We have three different types of suites available. There's the penthouse suites, business suites and the honeymoon suites." She winks. "Which one are you looking to book and for how long?"

"I'm not sure how long we'll be here but best to make it a couple of weeks for now. And we'll take the honeymoon suite thank you." Batting my eyes at her, I cuddle into Quinn's arm. He stiffens against my touch.

"Relax, it's for appearances only. Now pretend we are in love okay?"

"Esmerelda, how are you—?"

"Telepathy numnuts. Now, act normal until I have booked and paid the receptionist."

"Wonderful, okay, so for 14 nights that comes to a total of $30,000. I'll just need some form of identification and your credit card to put on the file please. This will be used for any charges made to your room, which will then be added to your card at the end of your stay."

The woman smiles widely, she is not well put together and the ghastly red lipstick that she's wearing has stained her teeth. Her hair is pulled back way too tight and it has stretched her skin taut, making her look like she's taken a ride on the Hollywood celebrity surgery train. I give her a polite smile and using my powers, create a credit card and drivers licence. I take it out of my purse and hand it over to the woman whose name tag states her name is Tiffany.

She taps away on her computer and once everything is finalised she hands me back my credit card and drivers licence, along with an electronic room key and a little paper slip which has the name of the suite on it and the password to the hotel's Wi-Fi.

"Okay, so the lifts are to the left there, you will need to use your room key to access your floor, just tap on the touch pad and then press the button to your floor. Your room is on the thirtieth floor. If you have any questions please don't hesitate to contact concierge."

She motions to someone behind me and next minute, there is a man dressed in a suit with a tag that says Trevor on it. "Good evening ma'am, Please allow me to take your luggage for you."

I give my thanks and, still clutching Quinn's arm, make my way to the left behind Trevor and into the elevator. I am thankful when we aren't greeted with the horrible sound of elevator music. I don't know what is with humans and their constant need to fill the void of silence with noise. I would much rather stand in an elevator in silence than listen to some stupid piano music. We finally arrive at my floor and the elevator doors open straight into my suite.

It is a sight to behold.

CHAPTER FIVE

I give an indulgent and satisfied smile, grateful I never have to worry about the issues of money, so I can live in luxury. I love the finer things in life, from luxury hotels to the little McMansion that I live in back in Sarria-Sant Gervasi. It's just one of the amazing perks of being a demon, and possessing a vessel that is sex on legs. Let's just say, there is rarely a time I have to pay for my own things. I'm smoking hot and I know it. I may seem like I'm up myself, but I'm just stating the truth. I'm blessed with a human with model good looks.

Quinn and I step out of the elevator, Trevor follows, rolling our luggage to the side and stands there, waiting patiently to be tipped for his service. I take some notes out of my purse and hand them to the bell boy who bows slightly and enters the elevator, leaving us alone.

"Wow," I breathe.

"Do you always waste your money on frivolous shit?"

Oh shut up assface.

"Yeah, what of it? I like the finer things in life, so sue me." I shrug.

I make a beeline for a set of double doors where I assume the bedroom will be. Opening them I am welcomed by the glorious sight of a king size bed with a chiffon and lace canopy.

I proceed to explore the rest of the massive room. Through another set of double doors to the left is the adjoining bathroom which has a spa bath.

I will definitely be enjoying you later.

On the other side of the room is a walk-in-closet. It is more impressive than mine at home. I don't have a shoe carousel, nor do I have a chaise in the middle where I can get ready.

"Are you done in there?"

I groan. "Yes, I'm coming." I snap back.

He can't give me a few minutes can he.

I walk into the open living/dining/kitchen area where Quinn is standing awkwardly at the dining table. He looks quite cute, unsure of what to do, a strained look on his face, trying to decide whether he should sit down or not. It's not something I expect to come from the big tough man.

"Okay let's regroup, right now we have the Book of the Dead… And that's it. We need to know where the gate is and what the three keys are. Since the demon back at the church was talking to Kane, that's exactly who I plan to summon."

"And what makes you think he'll talk?"

Seductively, hips swinging from side to side, I walk up to

him. "Because." I lean in really close, so close that my lips brush his ear lightly. "I can be *very* persuasive." I say ever so softly.

An audible gulp can be heard. Oh, how delightful. It seems that I affect Quinnie boy in more ways than one. A smile creeps up on my face.

I move over to the living room and shift the coffee table from its position by flicking my finger in the direction that I want it to move.

I snap my fingers and a mat with a pentagram and runes written on the outside appear along with some symbols written a few centimetres from that. This is my trap for Kane. I speak the words of the summoning spell, repeating it a few times as is required.

Nothing.

"Good job, maybe the spell is broken." He says sarcastically. Ignoring him, I wait a few more minutes, but again, nothing.

"Son of a bitch!" I exclaim, spinning on my heels and storming off.

"Do you kiss your mother with that mouth?" A deep voice asks.

Kane. How nice of you to drop by.

"Well, it's about time." I spin around. Damn, he's chosen a good-looking vessel, unlike the one I had seen before in the other demon's memories. A thatch of dark brown hair which is slicked back, sapphire blue eyes with flecks of hazel. He is definitely a sight, not as good looking as Quinn, but I'd say close enough.

"No, definitely not as good looking as Quinn." Vee adds. "Though, I have yet to find anyone as good looking as Quinn. When did gargoyles get so hot?!"

"This is so unlike you Vee, you're usually the prude."

"I'm not a prude!" Vee's voice becomes high pitched as she defends herself. "I love men, just because I don't jump every guy I see!"

"Is that meant to be an insult? Because I'm not insulted. I love men and I love sex. It's natural."

"What do you mean it's about time? It's been a few minutes. God you're impatient." I snap back to the real world and out of my own head.

"Well I'm sorry, but time is factor. I hear you are the demon to talk to about a plan to release Malphas from his fortress."

"What's it to you?"

"Does that really matter?"

Kane shrugs. "No, but I would like to know."

"Have you heard of this plan?" I throw back, completely ignoring his question.

"No."

Oh for fuck sake.

My power flows out and wraps itself around his neck, strangling him where he stands. Kane clutches his throat, gasping for breath.

"Are you going to quit lying to me, or will we be here all day?"

He makes a gurgling sound, trying to talk so I release my power's grip, allowing him to speak.

"Fuck you."

He manages to say before I exhale and tighten my grip on his neck, watching his face turn blue.

"No thanks, you aren't my type. Now, let me tell you how this is going to go. You *will* tell me who is behind this. How, is up to you. This can be done, as they say, the easy way, or the hard way. You either just give me the information I need or I force it out of you. And believe me, you don't want the latter." I release my grip on his neck a little and walk to stand in front of him. "Now, what's it going to be?"

He spits in my face. "Fuck you."

I wipe the spittle from my face as my true demonic side comes out. It's a side that I have not used for a long time. Since being out of the demon game, I have no need to use it. Yeah, traces of it show every now and then, when I get pissed off, but nothing like this. My demonic side is a sadistic and cruel mistress who takes pleasure in the torture of others. It is almost out of instinct. My arm shoots out burying deep into his body, and grips his heart, squeezing it tight. Kane cries out in pain, his knees buckle for a moment before he straightens back up again. A look of pain replacing the smug look on his face.

"Tell me what you know about the plan to release Malphas from his fortress!" I shout.

"This is going well isn't it?" Quinn sniggers.

"Oh shut it Quinnie boy."

"Don't call me that." His voice is dark, deep and gravelly, he sounds incredibly sexy which sends shivers through me, making me wish we were alone.

This is not the time to be having these thoughts about the gargoyle Esmerelda!

Vee giggles.

"Okay, I'll tell you." Kane says, his face still contorted in pain.

Turning my attention back to Kane, remove my hand from his body and grab a hand towel from the kitchen, wiping my arm. "I'm so happy that you have come to your senses with this. Now let's start again!" I say cheerfully like I wasn't just wrist deep inside his chest. "Who is behind this?"

"I don't know who is, but I do know that it is all in motion." His voice strains as he attempts to get his breathing back to normal, hand clutching his chest.

"How close are they to releasing him?"

"They need to find a main gate to the Underworld, the three keys and the book of the dead."

"How close are they to finding the location?"

A deafening silence greets me, the air is thick with it.

CHAPTER SIX

Several minutes pass and still no answer from Kane. His piercing obsidian eyes are focused on me like a laser as I contemplate my next move. I can't go any more demon than I already have, it's hard to come back from it. I know it seems that I've gone full demon, but this is nothing. The torture, the pain inflicted, all of this. Nothing, compared to how bad I can go.

I walk up and yank his arm, twisting it at the same time. Kane wails in pain, which sounds more like a female fox's mating call. I wince from the excruciating sound that assaults my eardrums.

"You aren't the first demon I have tortured and you certainly won't be the last. Now for shit's sake, tell me what I want to know!"

"Fine!" Kane says, hunches over and pops his shoulder back into place. "We have narrowed down the location of the gate to the Underworld to three locations. The Washington

Cemetery, A haunted house on Beckett Street and The Church of Notre Dame. The keys to unleashing Malphas haven't been figured out yet."

"The Church of Notre Dame?" Quinn asks softly.

I look up at him, knowing exactly what he is thinking, it's the same thing I am. What if it is the church, and the demons already know? The main gate to the Underworld would give off a rather powerful energy, like a beacon, and if they have sensed it then all they would need to do is get the book and the three keys. It will be a dark day for humanity if Malphas comes back to Earth.

I didn't sense anything at the church, so I don't think the church is it.

Malphas is the most fucked up of Lucifer's soldiers. His first in command Satan, most commonly mistaken by humans as being Lucifer himself, is a psycho motherfucker, but none matched up to that of Malphas. He is in his own realm of crazy that one.

"Yes, you know that building where *God*," he says, making air quotes with his fingers. "lives."

"I know the church scumbag—" Quinn barks out.

"Ooo, big words for the pathetic human." Kane turns to face me. "Really? This guy? You've turned away from your fellow brethren to help these hapless losers? The others are going to love this."

"The others aren't going to find out." I feel my power curl itself around his heart and with a simple thought I tug on the end of the tether. Kane falls to his knees, struggling to keep himself up as I tug on the tether a little more. I'm uncaring, cruel, I can feel my demonic side rising further up, just like when I had plunged my hand deep into his body, enjoying the feeling of the blood dripping down my arm, his heart in my hand.

Back in the day, I was known as the Black Widow. And no, I didn't fuck guys and then kill them. I used my assets, my skills, my seductive nature to get what I wanted and then kill with no remorse. I loved the kill, hungered for it. I was one of Lucifer's best weapons, so kicking that habit took a lot out of me. I was an addict, trying to kick hard drugs.

I fell off the band wagon so many times because I couldn't handle the pain, the torture and the restless nights, until I came across a shaman. He fixed me right up and gave me a soul. I know, how *Buffy the Vampire Slayer* does that sound? The only difference between myself and the painfully annoying Angel from the TV show, is that I wanted it to happen.

A soft hand lands on my shoulder bringing me back to reality. I look up at Quinn, and instantly get lost in his beautiful blue eyes. All I can think about is how his eyes are drilling into me, travelling down my face and straight to my lips, quickly, but enough for me to notice and savour the moment. My eyes roam his face, his oh so perfect face. I drink in every inch of him. His strong jaw, 5 o'clock shadow and plump, kissable lips. He is an Adonis that's for sure. I can't be thinking about how he makes me feel, the warmth that is quickly spreading, covering every inch of my body, making me yearn for his hard. . . .

Snap out of it!

"You okay there Dee?" Vee asks, amused.

"Yes, I'm fine Vee. Totally okay."

I release my hold on the tether.

"What do you say? Do I have to worry about you or not?" I ask Kane.

He looks up at me with pleading eyes. I love when they have that look of desperation, begging me to not continue with my torture. I don't know what he's worried about. I haven't gone nearly as hard on him as I did with the first demon back in Spain. I've reigned back my torture.

I bend down so that Kane and I are face to face and place a hand on his shoulder. He flinches. "Good, I'm glad I don't have to worry about you. But, just to be sure," I start to say before I'm interrupted by Kane.

"Just kill me already if that's what you plan to do."

I bring my index finger and tap my lips while feigning deep thought. "I was going to, but I have a *much* better idea."

I place my hand on the back of his neck and mutter a spell. He twitches under my touch.

"What was that!" A yelp forces its way out of his mouth. I smother a laugh that is fighting to break free from me. It's not every day you see a demon yelping like a puppy.

"I marked you. You will act as my little informant, getting me the information that I need from your buddies down in the Underworld and report back to me.

If I find that you have lied to me, double crossed me or, told *anyone* that you have spoken to me, well, you will be brought to me straight away where I will proceed to torture you. Slowly, continuously, aggressively. All of which will go on for days, making you beg for death. I will slow your healing abilities down slightly, so it takes you longer and you can feel the pain for longer. I am accustomed to torture tactics and will *not* hesitate to use them before I kill you, cockroach. Have I made myself perfectly clear?"

His Adam's apple bobs up and down, the classic response to fear in a male. Men are strong and pigheaded, always trying to save face and never wanting to seem weak, but their Adam's apple can give away so much about how they are feeling. I relish this, bathe in it. Completely satisfied I stand up, help him back up on his feet and release him from the trap. With a wave of my hand, I send him back to wherever he came from.

"We've got work to do."

CHAPTER SEVEN

"The sun's about to come up."
I stare out the window and see the faintest reddish orange glow out on the skyline. I nod in acknowledgement and walk over to the kitchen.

"So, how does this work exactly? Is it a Cinderella thing where you have to be back in your tower on time or you just go poof from wherever you are?"

"I just disappear from wherever I am."

"Geeze, you'd never want to be in the middle of sex when that happens. The poor woman."

"Poor woman?"

"Man?" I ask, raising an eyebrow.

"I would never put myself in that situation with a woman to just *"poof"* as you so eloquently put it." He snaps at me

"Oh for fuck sake, settle down, I'm being facetious."

I conjure up a bottle of chilled Brown Brothers Cienna. I've done a fair amount of travelling in my time, needing to be on the move often so as to not be caught by Lucifer's goons. I had travelled to Australia a few times. Beautiful country, very warm. My kind of weather, very tropical, like being in the Mediterranean. You can keep to yourself if you want, people rarely got to know their neighbours.

I had plans to move there before all of this shit happened. If I survive… If we survive all this, I will make the move to Australia and live in Sydney, maybe by the water, or on one of the little islands that surrounded the country.

I unscrew the bottle and grab a glass from the cupboard. Hesitating, I look from the bottle, to the glass and then back again and shrug.

Ahhh, fuck it.

Bringing the bottle to my lips, I savour the sweet taste of the deliciously chilled red, allowing the flavours of grapes, strawberry and cherry to dance on my tongue and awaken my tastebuds as the wine makes its way down my throat. I close my eyes and cherish the deliciousness, licking my lips and moaning softly.

Quinn is staring at me when I open my eyes, his eyes hooded, holding a distinct look of desire. He quickly turns his attention to my laptop when he notices that I have caught him red handed checking me out. I continue to swig the wine from the bottle as I walk back to him. I know, real lady-like right? Drinking alcohol straight from the bottle. I might as well park myself on the curb and be done with it.

After polishing off the whole bottle in a matter of minutes I set it down on the dining table and take a seat next to him.

"So, game plan. I can check out each of the locations in the day and see if I get a feel of dark energy from either of the sites. If I get a hit then we can go there at night, once you materialise into a human… errr, humanoid? Your non-stone self… again."

"I would like to go with you to each of the locations but I guess considering the tight timeline we have, this is the best and most viable option."

"Good, I'm glad we are in agreeance with each other."

"But, if you screw with me—"

I hold my hand up, motioning him to stop talking. "Just calm down there Quinnie boy. I'm not going to scew you over. We are on the same side, regardless of what you think of my kind, I am *not* the bad guy here. I think I've proved that enough already by saving your ass twice."

"Just don't screw me over, it's a friendly warning." He grumbles.

I get up from my seat and deposit the empty wine bottle in the recycling bin. Yes, I, a demon, like to recycle and protect the Earth from dying. This time, I choose to have a Moscato Riesling. I turn around to offer Quinn a glass, but he's gone.

No warning or anything.

This is going to be so much fun, I think sarcastically.

CHAPTER EIGHT

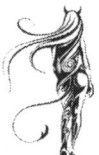

I stare up at the wrought iron gates of the old cemetery. Quinn and I had agreed the night before that I would take a look at the various sights of potential main gates to the Underworld. The gates are no longer open, they were shut down by angels long ago to prevent a disaster of epic proportions from happening.

I enter and wander around, feeling for the particular energy that would leak off a gate to the Underworld. I pass headstone after headstone all lined up one after each other, feeling nothing. Some had flowers placed in front of the headstone and some people were visiting loved one's graves and talking to the deceased.

They're never going to get the message.

Their spirits can't hear what the person is saying, they are either up in heaven or down in the pits of the Underworld. The only ghosts that ever stuck around were the ones that refused to cross over, the ones that somehow evaded the

Grim Reaper's grasp. They were usually people that had died in a horrific way, had unfinished business or were damn pissed off.

A dark energy catches my attention, it's very faint and I'm lucky I'm able to sense it. It is coming from a mausoleum and I stalk toward it like it owes me money. You can tell it was built years ago, it's old and falling apart. It looks like a house and on top sits a cross.

I never understood why people put so much faith in a deity that couldn't care less whether his creations lived or died. And no, I'm not talking about the wars, illnesses, famine and all that lot. They are necessary, if there was none of it, the world would be overpopulated and everyone would be living in desolate wastelands. Those would seem like a walk in the park and minor in comparison.

I'm talking about demons roaming the Earth, possessing and killing humans. He doesn't give a shit, yet people still pray to him like he is going to suddenly get off his high horse and help them. All he does is sit up there, looking down on everyone with a feeling of indifference.

Okay, in all honesty, I had no idea what he was doing up there, but that's the image I have in my head. He is a little child who has grown tired of their toys and created things to shake things up. Try telling that to these fools and they get all huffy and basically come at you with pitchforks and torches, a real lynch mob situation.

It was from that point that I learnt that religion is never to be discussed. People generally don't like it when you call them idiots and tell them that their saviour is a sadistic fucker that doesn't actually care what happens to them and that he probably is in cahoots with his beloved fallen son Lucifer.

Yeah, never go and discredit their beloved "Father".

I push open the heavy-set door to the mausoleum. Lining the walls on each side are torches. I can feel the energy becoming stronger and stronger the further I venture in, although still not as strong as it should be. The only sound is the echo of my shoes on the stone floor.

I enter the only room situated at the end. The only thing inside is a single concrete coffin, the lid sitting slightly askew. Treading lightly to the centre of the room, I take a moment to feel for the energy which leads me to the coffin.

"The gate can't be in the coffin. Maybe there's a secret door or something." Vee says.

"That's what I'm thinking."

I place a gentle hand on the cold stone wall and run my hand along it as I walk around, feeling for a little give in the stonework that'll suggest a secret room.

After feeling around and finding nothing, I walk over to the coffin and push the lid back. The stench of rotting corpse assaults my senses. The kind of smell that could literally peel the skin off your bones. Instead of there being the skeleton of a deceased human, there is a set of steps leading to an underground room.

"What's the go with the stairs?" Vee asks.

"I don't know. It's not something you find in a coffin, let alone a mausoleum. The only thing I can think of is that the mausoleum was built on top of whatever is down there."

I jump over the wall of the coffin and head down the steps. I don't have to go far before I reach the bottom. It isn't the best welcome. Lying on the ground, rotting away and looking like zombies, are six humans. None of them had managed to get to the stairs to escape, not that it would be been possible to even if they had. It looks like these guys were trying to summon a demon, judging by the pentagram on the wall.

I examine the bodies closer, it's like the demon they summoned had been struck by the muse of creativity. Each one has been killed a different way. One has blood seeping from its eyes, so much that the only thing you can see is red. Another has a hole in its chest cavity, and the middle section of its ribcage ripped out, leaving splintering along the remainder of the ribs. Organs splayed out, half hanging out of the person and a massive pool of dried blood sitting beneath them. Whoever the demon was, it went to town on these poor saps. None of them stood a chance against it.

Humans always thought they knew how to summon demons and what they were getting into. The stories told at church are nothing like what the reality is. Demons are brutal. They have little regard nor hold any emotion for those around them, especially for those they feel are beneath them. They are cooped up in the Underworld, so when summoned by stupid humans they let loose and wreak havoc, leaving a trail of corpses in their path.

Carefully walking through the piles of bodies I keep my attention on the pentagram placed on the wall. The energy that is being emitted from the pentagram is of dark energy, but not the one that is a gateway to the Underworld. I crack the pentagram on the wall making it unusable for any future summons.

I take out the map I had bought with me from my back pocket, marked with the places that I needed to travel to.

Next stop on the gateway to hell tour. Haunted house.

CHAPTER NINE

So this is the most haunted house on the East Coast of America hey? It doesn't look too haunted to me, just old and run down.

I step through the metal gates that surround the circumference of the Victorian style home. Curious about its history, I had done a bit of research, and according to Google the home had been abandoned a long time ago. The previous residents left when the woman of the house went mad with rage and murdered her entire family. She apparently had no prior conditions of insanity or any other mental illnesses that would induce a sudden breakdown in her mental state. Like making her go bat shit crazy on her family and chop them up into little pieces before burning their remains in the fireplace. The reports state that she advised the cops she was possessed, that she knew everything that was happening but could do nothing to stop it.

The courts had deemed her insane and not fit for release

into the real world. There were over 20 cases like these which showed residents of the home being driven to insanity due to the "devil".

I stare up at the dilapidated old house with the gutter hanging low, which is only connected by a thin piece of metal. A light gust of wind will have it tumbling to the ground. The grass is so old and dry that there is no way to revive it back to its healthy and green state. The overgrown dead trees look more like old, wrinkly fingers than actual branches as they twist and turn around the pillars of the front balcony of the home. The windows are smashed in and there is graffiti all over, most of it crudely drawn pictures or curse words. There were some pentagrams along with stupid shit like "The devil rules" and "hail Satan". I'll never understand humans and their obsession with Lucifer.

The energy from this house is extremely strong, it kisses my skin, the all too familiar tingling feeling of absolute power. I don't know whether that is from the high spirit energy from the house or whether it's because the gate is here. I'm about to head to the stairs when someone grabs me by the shoulders. I spin around quickly, slamming them against the iron fence. The culprit lets out a hiss of pain as I allow the dark power to rise up to the surface.

"What do you want?" I spit out.

"I-I-I-I'm..."

"Well spit it out, I don't have all day"

"I-I-I-I was going to tell you not to go into the house man. P-P-P-Please don't hurt me!" the man wails. He whimpers like a scared little puppy, shrinking down to make himself look less of a threat to me. I let go of his shirt and brush him off.

I give him the most sheepish look I can muster without it making me want to vomit from the sheer act of it. "I'm so sorry about that, you just took me by surprise." I let out a nervous chuckle.

Ugh, this is so degrading.

I hate human emotions, they always get in the way. Ever since I rescued my vessel from sure death, I had to fight off a flood of emotion from her and everyone who had obviously known that her husband was a psychotic dick. It's the reason I moved away from her little Gitano clan and ventured out on my own. They started doing my head in with all of their crap.

"It's okay, I'm fine. Why are you going into that house anyway? A girl like you should be out celebrating the day like the rest of America, not venturing into a haunted house."

"That's none of your business."

I start to walk off before he grabs me by the arm. I look down to where he has his hand before looking up and shooting him a 'really? after last time?' look. Realising what he's done, he quickly removes his hand from my arm like it's on fire.

"I seriously don't think you should go in there." He sounds desperate to try and stop me.

"This guy is kind of annoying." Vee's annoyance is clearly showing in her tone.

"I know right? Would it be bad if I just teleported him somewhere else?" I ask.

"Yes! Don't do that, remember that you aren't evil anymore and you are trying to coexist with humans. That means NOT messing with them." She scolds me like I'm a kid that has just done something naughty.

He pleads with me to not enter. The poor sap looks genuinely scared. I look into his eyes and using my ability of mind control I compel the guy to move on.

"You will leave me and this place right now. You never saw me; do I make myself clear?"

"Didn't I say not to mess with humans Dee?!" Vee shouts.

"Well what do you suggest I do? Huh?"

"Ummm..."

"Exactly."

He indicates his understanding and without a word, leaves the premises, heading to the city. I walk up the stairs to and grab a hold of the door knob and push it slowly. It creaks against the rusted-out hinges. There is darkness all throughout. I thought the exterior of the home looked like shit, well, it is nothing compared to the inside. It seems that the trees wanted to be the new residents of the home and a couple of them have sprouted in various spots.

I follow the energy pulsating from the house, the feeling of it is exhilarating as it roils through me, awakening all my senses. I walk into the kitchen and then into what could have been mistaken for a closet. The basement.

Typical.

The timber stairs creak beneath me as I make my way down. Walking off to the right I find the spot the dark energy is emanating from. There is no pentagram with runes surrounding it, the energy is purely from the presence of ghosts in this house. There is a malevolence here, there is no doubt about that, but not the kind I'm looking for. I search the rest of the home, in case the gate is in a different part of it, but come up short.

This only leaves the church.

I have to be careful teleporting there this time, it's daylight and full of people. Closing my eyes once more I teleport myself behind the church where there is a less of a chance of being spotted by unsuspecting humans. I make my way to the front and I'm immediately grateful for my decision. The courtyard is bustling with people setting up for some kind of festival. Chairs and tables are being set up at the far end, the various restaurants and other businesses setting up banners from the overhang of their shops. A stage is being set up in front of the church steps with crew members grunting and people giving directions on where to put various parts of the stage.

I've seen a lot of churches. *A lot*. And after you've seen one you've pretty much seen them all. But this one is quite a church and I can't help but admire it. I know right, a demon admiring a church. Laughable. It's massive and looks like there were actually two little churches combined to make the one church. There are a lot of columns that are attached with a walkway which connects them. Sticking up from the middle behind the walkway is a bell tower, and below that, a little window. Perched along the ledge around the church are gargoyles, looking menacing as they overlook the city, with one big gargoyle in the centre.

The one in the middle is less hideous than its buddies and my thoughts trail off to Quinn, the gargoyle I had met yesterday. It doesn't look a thing like him. It isn't tall and handsome like he is, but short and stumpy like most gargoyles, just to a larger scale. Its face is harsh, mouth open with fangs jutting menacingly out. Its wings are tucked in a little behind it and the way it leans over in a crouched position gives the impression of a hunched back.

I step into the small entrance that I had teleported myself into the night before and make my way into the main area. Stained glass windows line the sides depicting the great accomplishments of God, Jesus and his many saints. There is a row of confession booths right at the entrance made of timber and stretching quite a few metres are rows and rows of pews. At the front of the church sits a marble table where the priest stands to spit out a whole bunch of drivel about God and his gloriousness and how caring and righteous he is.

Standing in the middle the isle in front of the table, I close my eyes to concentrate on sensing any darkness. At first I feel nothing, then comes the faintest of darkness seeping through, slithering its way through the church like a worm. I open my eyes and follow it to a door to the right, the energy becomes stronger as I get closer to it.

This is a different feeling to what I sensed in the cemetery and the haunted house. This dark energy comes to me in waves, pulsating, though it still has a strong sense of malevolence to it. I can feel it tainting my very soul, threatening to turn it black again. There is no mistaking that this is the gate to the Underworld. Who'd-a thunk it. A main gate to the Underworld located within a church of Christ. It is just dripping with irony.

I'm about to jiggle the door knob to see if it is unlocked when a male voice speaks to me. "Can I help you there miss?"

My head shoots in the direction of the stranger's voice. Standing there is a priest, dressed in simple black trousers and button up shirt with a white clerical collar.

Time to play the sweet and innocent little human.

"No Father, I just came to check out one of the most beautiful churches I have ever seen." I lean in and whisper. "And I have seen *a lot* of churches." He gives me a look to say he isn't inquiring about my presence in the church but my interest in the room I'm standing in front of. "Oh, sorry about this Father, I was hoping to find you, actually, well not you specifically, but a priest, as I have some questions."

He relaxes at my beautiful lie, giving me a warm and gentle smile. "Sorry my dear. I was just in my office doing some work, I didn't hear you come in I'm afraid.

"Oh no that's fine, I can be pretty quiet." I let out a chuckle that sounds like wind chimes singing in a breeze.

"So, what would you like to know dear?

"I just wanted to ask some questions regarding the history of the church Father—?"

"Father Frollo."

"Father Frollo, nice to meet you." I extend my hand in an invitation to shake, which he obligingly accepts. "Like I said, I've been to many churches and you rarely find ones that still hold this gothic design, especially with the gargoyles on top.

"This is an old church and has been around since the dark ages. It is very lucky to have the council on its side to maintain it though."

"I'm glad, a church like this should be kept in tip top condition. So nothing was here before the erection of the church would that be right?"

He thinks for a moment than says. "Not that I know of my dear."

"How long have you been serving at this church father?"

"I'm relatively new here, I took over from the last priest who is now retired."

"So it's safe to assume you don't know much on its history?"

"That's right. All I know is that this church gets busy during the special holidays and that we have a mass tonight, if you would like to attend." He offers.

"What time would that be?"

"6:00pm, during the Halloween celebrations outside.

I think back to the set up that is happening.

So that's what all that is for.

"Oh, so that's what is going on out there. Interesting. So what happens on Halloween here?"

"Parents take their kids out for trick or treating and come here to party with the rest of the community. Every year they hold the festivities in the courtyard. There are games for everyone and lots of food and drinks."

"Oh wow!" I express excitement.

"So, will you be attending the festivities with the rest of them?"

"Oh I don't know, I've only just arrived in this town, I don't even have a costume and I'm sure all the good ones would have been taken from the shops already."

"Oh come on Dee! Let's have some fun! I miss celebrating Dia De Los Muertos! This is the closest thing to it! Pleeeeeease."

"Quiet down!" I hiss.

"Well, if you are a tourist here, then you must join in on the festivities. There is a shop just down the road where you will still find some costumes, they are our biggest costume store, so you are bound to find something that'll take your fancy."

"Please don't take this as an offence Father, but I'm surprised that you would be into an event such as Halloween, considering what it celebrates."

"I'm not an old Father, I am hip with the times." He lets out a light chuckle.

Halloween is a frivolous exercise. No matter what you called it and no matter where you celebrate it. The innocent go about their daily lives thinking that Halloween is just some celebration where they can let their inhibitions go and dress up as something scary, when in fact all it does is give us free reign to fuck shit up. We run rampant at this time of year. Halloween has the highest crime rate annually and yet the humans still don't believe in the monsters that lurk in the shadows.

Lucifer had one thing right when he spoke about the humans, they are dumb as shit and so naive to what is really around them. I guess ignorance is bliss. I don't want to attend this stupid tradition.

I groan inwardly. I'm going to have to attend this piss shit celebration.

"Well, I guess it does sound pretty wonderful, and I don't have any plans tonight. Okay, I'll go, I'll check out the costume store on the way back to my hotel. Thank you Father, what's the name of the store?"

I feel Vee jumping around and shouting and I can't help but feel happy for her. I like my vessel and I never give her any time to just be here and take control of her own body, so I'm glad that I can at least give her something.

"It's called All Things Heavenly and Devilish."

CHAPTER TEN

I look at myself in the mirror. Using my powers, I have conjured up the most perfect costume for me, inspired by Vee's lineage.

I'm wearing a veil skirt with deep fuchsia pink as the base and curtains of yellow, orange, purple and pink which is lined with sequins and little gold coins hanging from the bottom. A thin chain belt of the same little gold coins attached to the skirt is hanging from my hip. I top it off with a sapphire blue corset which tied up at the back and a loose white blouse, matching it with a nice purple scarf that I use as a headband. I puff up my black curly hair more, making it all poofy and big.

The whole look is perfect. I don't know why, but I'm actually excited about this. I take one last look at myself, do a little twirl, and then teleport back to the courtyard. I don't worry about appearing out of nowhere. I know it will be super busy and that nobody is actually going to take any notice of me, not today of all days

The courtyard is packed full of people who are milling around, drinking and having a great time with friends and family. There are little children running about, squealing. I watch them do their thing, wide smiles plastered on their faces as they play gleefully with other kids. They are dressed in a mix of different mythological creatures from Frankenstein's monster to werewolves and everything in between.

I smile as a group of kids run around me giggling their delight. A little girl, dressed in a similar costume stops in front of me, her eyes going wide as she looks me up and down, noticing that I am dressed the same as her. She grabs my skirt with her chubby little hand and tugs at it, giving me a big toothy grin.

"We are dressed the same!" She speaks loudly, her cute little squeaky voice warming my heart. I fight the tears that threaten to escape.

"Are you okay Dee?" I feel Vee's concern at my sudden emotional state.

"Yeah, I'll be fine."

"Well I'm here if you need me."

"Thank you Vee." I'm grateful for her concern.

"That we are little one." I smile down at her, my voice a little strained.

I bend down so we are eye level, that way she doesn't have to strain her neck to look at me.

"Uh huh!" She moves from side to side, her dress swaying

as she does. "Gypsies are so pretty and they wear pretty dresses and are so pretty!"

"Romani, they don't like to be called gypsies." She looks at me with a confused look on her face. I clear my throat. "I mean, they're not as pretty as you." I pet her head and she giggles.

"My name is Isabella! What's your name?!"

"Nice to meet you Isabella, my name is Esmerelda." I hold my hand out and she takes it in hers, shaking it vigorously. "And how old are you Isabella?"

"I am." She looks at her left hand and with her right index finger counts how old she is. "I am four years old!" She exclaims loudly and proudly, a wide smile on her face. "I'm a big girl now!"

"Yes, yes you are. Are you having a good time?"

"Yep!" She looks around, brows furrow, looking worried as she realises that her friends are no longer around. "I have to find my friends!" She shrieks. "Bye! Have fun Esme. . . Esme. . . Esmella!" She says awkwardly, running off.

I watch her leave, a sudden feeling of sorrow filling my heart and for the first time, tears start trickling down my cheeks.

"I didn't realise that you were the type to dress up for Halloween." The delectable baritone voice of Quinn floats down to me. I blink wildly, wiping away the tears that manage to escape.

"Well, we've only just met, there's a lot of things that you don't know about me like—" I stop short when I stand up and see him.

Quinn is dressed well, which is a very bad thing for me, cause he's dressed up as Clark Kent. He's superman. My favourite superhero, which is purely based on Henry Cavill, who is amazingly hot. He's wearing black slacks, a white dress shirt that is unbuttoned up the top, showing off a bit of the skin-tight Superman top underneath. It is so skin tight I can see his pecks through the dress shirt. He's even topped it off with glasses and his hair is styled.

Fuck he looks fucking hot, I just want to... *Oh shit, you need to get laid woman.*

I can't stop my eyes from roving all over his body and landing right on his crotch. Damn I would love to find out what is underneath those slacks. Not for the first time, I picture his hard cock driving deep into me as I scream out his name. I'm happy to find that the look on his face mirrors mine. His eyes hooded and his breath is laboured. I watch him as his eyes go from my lips, neck and straight to my breasts which are pushed so far up, they're popping out of my corset, looking like they're trying to escape the confines of said corset.

He blushes a little when he realises I've been watching him eye humping me.

"See something you like?" I croon

"Hmmm. . ." He looks at his watch. "It's 6:30pm, the last mass service has been on for half an hour, so we have a couple of hours give or take. Father Frollo usually stays at the church for an hour after a service to tie things up. I guess we could mill around with the rest of the people." He says, ignoring my question.

Surprisingly I feel hurt that he doesn't answer my question. What is wrong with me? I can't be feeling this way towards him. Nothing would or could happen between us, he is a gargoyle who turns to stone during the day, and whilst I like my men to be as hard as stone, I don't want their entire body to be that way.

I decide to brush it all off.

"Well not being from the area and having never been to one of these, what do you recommend we do?"

"I have never been to one of these before either so I would have no idea."

"But you dressed up?" Confused at his statement.

"Well it is a lot easier to blend in this way." He states nonchalantly.

"Okay, so why don't we just walk around and see if there is anything that takes our fancy?"

He nods in agreement and leads the way.

CHAPTER ELEVEN

We spend the next hour walking around, checking out the various food stalls that are lined up on the perimeter of the courtyard. We finally settle on having Gyros from the Greek stall, and after grab ourselves a drink from the bar, me, a whiskey neat and him, boring ass soda.

We find ourselves a bench and sit down. A painfully awkward silence passes between us. I don't know what to say or do, I feel awkward being around him now and there is a weird sensation in my stomach.

"That's butterflies sweetie." Vee pipes up.

"What?"

"Butterflies. You feel for Quinn. It's actually kind of cute seeing you this way."

"Uuughh. I don't have butterflies!"

"Dee's in love." Vee sing songs.

"Shut up!" I throw her into her little room and focus on

the situation at hand.

"What's it like being a gargoyle? Doesn't it get tiresome, shifting into stone at the end of the night?"

"No, I've been like this for quite a few years now, it's second nature to me."

"What do you mean you've been like this for a few years? I thought you were born like this."

"Ahhh, yeah, yeah I was." He says, tripping over himself.

"Then why—"

"I don't want to talk about it."

"I'm sor—"

"I said drop it!" He yells so loudly that several people look in our direction and scowl at him.

"I don't know what your problem is. I ask you a simple fucking question 'cause stupidly thought that we could get to know each other. I know you hate me because of what I am, you've made that perfectly clear, but we agreed to work with each other. So could you for once act normal instead of being hot and cold?!" I blow up at him.

"What happens now? You whinge and whine about it and then start crying?" His voice dead and emotionless.

Without realising it and based purely on instinct, I punch him straight on the jaw. "I'm not some pathetic human, gargoyle, I don't go around wallowing in self-pity and start acting like that crazy singer who keeps bitching in her songs about guys not giving her any attention or fucking her over. All I'm asking is that you act like a decent person and treat me with the same respect I have given you! But if you find it difficult to even show a shred of decency, I will do this without your help."

Not wanting his answer I storm off, heading into the densely populated courtyard, hiding myself in the crowd. I don't want him anywhere near me, I don't understand what the issue is with him. A simple question has him acting like a dick. Why do I even care? I've just met him.

A tear rolls down my face.

Oh great, and now I'm acting like a chick in every romcom ever made.

I don't know what it is about this guy that has me feeling things I have never felt about anyone before. I don't get emotional like this. I can feel the anger and sadness well up inside me at a quick pace, ready to break free like a geyser. When I reach the other side of the courtyard I keep on walking, ending up at the side of the church. My power is boiling and if I don't release it soon I'm going to explode and there will be trouble. I push my hands out, letting out a wave of energy and destroying a sign ahead of me. I watch it fly off in all directions and little remnants of it float down softly like snow.

Breathing heavily, I feel a hand land on my shoulder. Grabbing it, I flip the person over and they land hard on the floor. I put my right pump on their throat, and look down to see that the person I have flipped is Quinn

"What do you want?" I'm very surprised at the calmness of my voice, considering how I'm feeling.

"I just. . ." He chokes out. I lift my shoe off his throat, he coughs out a bit and rubs his throat. "I want to apologise for my behaviour tonight.

"Oh really? The demon hunter wants to apologise to the lowly demon? I thought I was beneath you."

He exhales. "I'm sorry Esme—"

"Don't call me Esme." My voice deep and ominous.

"So, what? You can call me Quinnie boy but I can't call you Esme?" He smirks.

I continue to scowl at him. *If you think that cracking a joke is going to get you back in my good graces, you have another thing coming Quinn.*

He clears his throat and stands up, brushing himself off. "I'm sorry Esmerelda, I'm not used to working with other ummm. . . . people let alone demons, and you aren't like any other demon I have ever come across. You aren't sadistic and made of pure evil. I don't know how to handle you."

"So you think acting like an ass is the best option?"

"It's hard, I do and don't trust you. There's a constant battle in my head on how to perceive you and I don't know what to do or think."

I relax a little and sigh. "Okay I get it. Demons aren't good, I know that, we are literally the scum of the Earth and I have not met many demons who turned out to be good. I will try and not take it personally and realise that you are trying to deal with a situation you have never been in."

"Wow Dee, how big of you." Vee says, surprised at my sudden change of emotion.

"I know, it's sickening."

"Thank you Esmerelda." Quinn sounds relieved that there isn't going to be a fight between us.

"You're welcome. Should we check out the church now?"

He looks at his watch and nod. "Yep, let's go. Follow me." He grabs my hand, and a warmth quickly spreads through me at his touch. He leads us back around to the front of the church, opens the doors with his keys and we walk in. Once inside, he releases my hand and I'm saddened at the loss of his warm skin.

"Where did you sense the dark energy from?" He asks quietly.

"In the room at the back there, to the right." I lead the way to the room and turn the door knob, surprised to find it open. I step in and feel around the wall like a blind person until my fingers land on the light, and I flick the switch.

There is a set of stairs that lead to a basement. *Again with the basements!* The light switch used to light the office also lights the basement. *Thank god*. The energy still isn't that strong and I pause for a moment. I can feel the distinct sensation of a containment spell. Someone or something has created a spell to hide the energy of this place. But why? I make my way down the stairs and when I reach the bottom and step through what I assume to be the wall of magic from the containment spell, I'm hit with a massive hit of dark power which nearly knocks me on my ass. I steady myself and allow it to course through me.

This church is definitely the location of the main gate, on the far wall there is an arched door with a padlock. All around the door there are runes. The air is thick with dark energy and it's like walking in jelly, or how I imagine it would be like to walk through jelly. Tentatively, I touch the door and instantly get thrown away, hitting the back wall. Groaning, I get back up and limp a little to Quinn. There is something odd about this one, I squint, stepping close to the door. Seeping out is a faint smoke of power, I watch it pass over me. I relish in the feeling, the feeling of obtaining little hits of extra power, and then something new snakes its way through the smoke. It's string like, light blue colour and it shimmers as it catches the light. This is a light power, one that is fighting the darkness. I recognise this as angelic power.

This would explain the containment spell and the angels didn't want the strong energy to be felt so they would have place this at the top of the stairs, though it seems like it has eroded over time. This doesn't help satiate the questions I have, it only raises more. Angelic power is powerful and shouldn't wear down overtime. So who or what has gotten to this? There is no way that a mid-level demon would have the power to do something like this. Which only suggests one thing, an upper-level demon is in town.

"We've found the main gate to the Underworld. We need to hurry, there's an upper-level demon in town. A containment spell has been placed on this basement but it's worn away, which is why I was able to walk through it."

"What makes you think that an upper-level demon is in town."

"Because the containment spell was created by an Archangel. Only Archangels have the power to lock the main gates to the Underworld, and only upper-level demons have the power to bring down an angel made spell. We should go back to the hotel, get the book and find a way to locate the keys."

"I agree." His lips move into a tight straight line. "Ummmm…"

"You'll be fine, it gets easier the more you teleport." I take his calloused hands into mine, looking deep into his eyes. The beautiful blue threatens to take me away to another place. I force myself to focus on the job at hand and take us to my hotel room. He handles it a lot better and it only takes a few minutes for him to recover.

We stay that way, fixated on each other. The world around us ceases to exist. His thumb circles lazily on my right palm. My breathing becomes rapid as his other hand lightly travels up my arm and lands on my cheek.

He closes the distance between us, my heart beating rapidly, it's so loud that I'm certain he can hear it pounding away like a jack hammer. I should stop whatever it is that is happening. This is not the time to be acting on my hormones right now. We should be finding out which upper-level demon is in town, but I can't stop, I press myself into him and his breath hitches. I lick my lips and follow the movement of his eyes as they fall on them.

H frowns. His facial expressions show his inner argument being played out in his head. This is wrong, we shouldn't be doing this. Before I can push him away, a low growl emanates from throat and his mouth slams down onto mine.

His kisses are exactly how I imagined them to be, desperate, passionate and hungry. His tongue traces my lips, nudging them, requesting entrance to which I oblige. Our tongues move together in a perfect synchronised dance. He is unbelievably amazing, lips so soft against my own. I'm heating up from just his kisses, a throbbing sensation which can be felt down in my core. Goosebumps scatter all over me.

If my temperature rises any further, then I'm going to set myself on fire. Never have I ever had anyone have such an effect on me. I don't know what it is about Quinn that gets me so worked up. I want more.

No, I need more.

I want to feel him.

All of him, inside of me, as I scream out his name in ecstasy, our bodies moving together as we ride each other hard.

I deepen my kisses and he reacts by lifting me up. I wrap my legs around him as he backs me up until we hit the dining table. Holding me up with one arm, he moves a chair aside with his other and then places me down.

The coolness of the timber table is a welcome change to my overly heated skin. I run my hand through his hair, squeezing my legs tighter around him. I moan into his mouth as I feel his rock hard cock pressed against my stomach.

"So this is where you've been." a female voice breaks through the sounds of our kissing.

Our attention is snapped away from each other as we

both look to the intruder that has interrupted our moment. Standing there with two beefed up steroid induced men is someone I never thought I would ever see again. Quinn and I separate quickly, like we are little kids who believe that cooties are real.

I smooth my skirt and glare at the bitch who has just ruined the hottest make-out session I have ever been part of.

"Abigail, what are you doing here? Tired of constantly being on your knees? It must be painful, being in that position all that time." A caustic tone coating my words.

"Oh *Esmerelda*, you pathetic little girl. What, you can't handle the rejection so you came up to this hole?"

"What do you want slut bag?" I sneer.

"You know what I want Esmerelda. . . Or, should I call you *Lilith*?" She accentuate my real name.

I let out a low growl.

"Lilith? As in Lucifer's lover?" Quinn asks incredulously.

Oh shit.

I look over at an irate Quinn. He thought so little of me before, but now? After finding out my real name, well, he is definitely going to try and do me in instead of do me.

CHAPTER TWELVE

"Yes, I am Lilith. But I'm no longer with that sadistic *fucker*. I left him centuries ago." I answer Quinn without looking at him, keeping my eyes on the demon in front of me. "And Abigail, if you really think that I'm just going to hand over the book, or that you are going to be able to rip it from my hands, then you are a just as much of a dipshit as you are a slut."

"Oooo, so hurtful Lil! Do I sense a hint of jealousy with those malicious words?" She croons.

I laugh out loud. "Jealous? Shit no! You can have him all to yourself! I wouldn't want him back if he was last demon on Earth! So go ahead, be my guest, take him as your lover. You two are actually perfect for one another."

"Well I'm glad to see you being so good about me being Lucifer's number one girl, and it looks like you have taken in a lover yourself. Although, I *am* surprised that you would take on a human to bang."

"We are *not* lovers." Quinn ground out.

"Naaaw, such a shame! You haven't changed a bit Lil, always screwing people over. Oh well! It's just like the saying, a leopard never changes its spots?" She laughed. "Okay, so, back to business. Give us the book, or you and your lover die."

"Oh yeah sure! I'll just go get it for you! Wait right there." I spit out a snarky response. I had placed the book in the hotel's safe, located in the walk-in wardrobe with a spell to hide it's location. I'm confident she won't find it.

I instantly felt a tightness around my throat. She is squeezing and squeezing, cutting the flow of oxygen into my lungs, I can already feel my windpipes bruising from her power. There are now tears, a steady stream of them falling down my cheeks. *I will not show you how much this is affecting me. I will not give you satisfaction of seeing me begging you to stop.*

An evil smirk appears on her face as she continues to squeeze the life out of me and I just want to smack that look off of her. I'm trying to get in as much oxygen as I possibly can but it isn't working. I start to see blackish grey spots as they pop up in my vision like fireworks. It eventually becomes too much and I drop to the floor. I look up to see Quinn looking down on me, uncaring, his eyes cold and dead.

Gone is the desire that had filled him only moments ago. The lust that was once evident in his beautiful baby blues had been eviscerated by a mere name. Lilith. Lucifer's former lover. We had just gotten to a good place, a really good place in fact. He no longer saw me as the evil soul sucking demon that he had to begin with. He looked at me in a new light, a light that painted me as a good being, someone he could picture being with. Abigail had ripped apart the beautiful relationship that was forming when she revealed my true identity. In this moment, I hate who I am.

Holding onto a string of hope, I give him a pleading look which doesn't change his mind, he just watches me being choked to death. Any further and Vee is going to die. I can't let her die. I saved her from an early death and like hell am I going to let this twatsicle be the one to take it away from her. She's disappearing, her life fading away, I can feel her struggle as she tries desperately to get a gulp of air into her lungs. We're working together to perform this simple task, yet are failing miserably.

I feel Vee giving up, letting go, and I try to keep my hold on her but it's no use. She's a human and doesn't have the resilience that demons do. She can't handle as much as I can. I have to do something, but before I can think of a plan to stop Abigail, the pressure in my head, chest, lungs and throat go away. The only evidence that I had just been choked is the dull ache in my head which is starting to float away.

I'm so thankful that as a top tier demon, I have the ability of self-healing. I mentally nudge Vee to see if she is still alive and a whisper of life greets me. I sigh in relief and place her on her bed in her little room. She's fragile and dainty, but the colour is returning to my skin, my breathing is becoming stronger. Not being able to handle the flood of emotions crashing down on me, I focus all that sadness and sorrow into unbridled anger.

"Come on now Lilith, do you really want to play this game?"

I look upon the she-demon who had my life in her hands, the permanent smug look on her face. "Eat a dick Abigail. That's what you're good at after all, isn't it?" My voice comes out strained and hoarse.

She stomps over, slapping me so hard on the face that I spit blood out.

"Boys, go find where the book is while I take care of this traitor right here."

Quinn flies into action but doesn't get far before he is frozen in place by Abigail, looking quite like those statues that you find on the main streets in the city. You know, the ones that are usually painted in silver or gold. You think they are actually a statue and then *Boom!* They spring to life and change positions or scare unsuspecting pedestrians.

Lucifer had definitely given the bitch a boost of power, she was never this strong before, she was just a lowly mid-level demon who craved power. I was always having problems with her trying to usurp me from my position as Lucifer's queen. She never wanted him for him, she only wanted power, she went mad for it. I showed her what would happen if she continued on with her pathetic vies for Lucifer's attention, but she was so determined – or stupid, I couldn't tell – that she had just kept on coming and coming. In the end I made her my little bitch and whenever I needed a stress release and Lucifer wasn't around, or I needed to take my anger out, I would use her, torturing her in ways that would impress the CIA.

"And where do you think you're going lover?" Her voice low and seductive.

She saunters over to Quinn, her small hand landing gently on his arm, lightly running it up, across his shoulder and then down his other arm. She leans in close and smells him, closing her eyes as she takes in the delicious scent.

"I understand why you would go for this human Lil, he smells delicious and he is very nice on the eyes. Seeing as though he seems to hate you right now, do you think I can have a go at him?"

She kisses him on the cheek, slowly working her way to his lips, looking at me she does it. She is goading me, trying to break me, showing me that she can take everything I have. I didn't love Lucifer when she had taken him, I wasn't even around when she did, but I wouldn't have cared then, and I don't care now. I was done with him the moment he hurt me. The simple act of showing authority, power and dominance over me.

I can see so much of him in Abigail, the way she shows off her undying power, the way she prances around like a fucking show pony, tail high in the air and head up, screaming out to the world, "look at me!". My jaw clenches as she continues her display of affection. When she reaches his lips, she gives him a quick peck. "Hmmm, this isn't as satisfying as I imagined it would be..." She snaps her fingers. "Of course! I know what is missing here!"

Abigail releases Quinn and says. "Kiss me lover."

He grabs her head and plants his lips on hers, kissing her passionately.

A pain like none I have ever felt before bubbles up inside my belly. I am fully aware that he is only kissing her because he is being compelled to, but I can't stop the hurt that is ripping through my heart. I'm experiencing the strangest mix of emotions. A real desire to end Abigail's life is filling me to the brim and combating the utter pain that has engulfed me.

"*You need to stop them.*" I'm elated when I hear Vee's voice enter into my consciousness. It's a little weak, but it's here, *she's* here.

"*I know.*" Is all I can say.

Right then, I make the stupid mistake of looking up, and that is when I snap. Somehow the anger that was fighting with the sadness to take primary residence in me has won. The scene being played out before me is practically a porno as Quinn has Abigail pinned against the wall. He is grinding against her, kissing her neck, Abigail is moaning loudly and when she catches me staring at them, she winks at me. Quinn stops kissing her long enough to take her top off and then proceeds to kissing her again. She is about to take off his slacks when I use every ounce of energy I have in me to throw Quinn off of her.

I send him sliding across the floor as I launch at Abigail like a wild animal. I grab her by the throat and throw her across the hotel room. Unperturbed, she jumps back up and pushes me against the wall. I push against her powers and meander over to her, not phased. She starts flinging various items at me which I easily deflect with my own powers.

"Abigail, we've got the book."

I whirl around. One of the goons is holding the Book of the Dead.

What the fuck! How the hell did they get passed my spell?!

The distraction is all Abigail needs to throw me across the room. My head, is the lucky one to meet the wall first, cushioning the blow for the rest of my body. I fall like a sack of potatoes, a sharp stabbing pain replacing the shooting pain through my head.

"Take the book to the boss now, he will be rather pleased that we have the book and the location of the main gate to the Underworld."

Her goons disappear as she turns to me. "Well, it's been a real pleasure Lil, and I'm terribly sorry, but I can't stick around. It's been fun catching up with you." She glides over to Quinn, who is still lying on the ground where I threw him.

She bends down and touches his shoulder.

"Stay away from him." I want it to be fierce, but instead it comes out as a poorly constructed threat. Slowly, I stand back up, stumbling my way towards her.

Abigail rolls her eyes.

She flicks her wrist, sending me flying out the window. The wind is whizzing past me, ruffling my hair as I plummet to the ground, buffeting in my ears, the sound becoming unbearable. I feel Vee panicking and I reassure her that she won't be dying, at least not tonight.

Using the last ounce of energy I have, I close my eyes and concentrate really hard, picturing my bed in the hotel room. I've been depleted of energy, but if I don't hurry up and get myself back in my room then I will have a painful greeting with the ground.

I try again and again, Vee now screaming at me as I fail to garner up enough energy inside of me to teleport in mid-air. I try again for the last time, but just as I feel myself floating up into the ether, I come crashing down onto a car.

I lay there, silent.

"V-V-V-Vee?" I stammer.

Silence. Nothing.

"Vee? Come on, talk to me."

Again, Silence. I listen intently for the slightest sound, but nothing. I've been concentrating that hard on listening out for it that I fail to notice the many people screaming at me to see if I'm okay.

Go away! Leave me alone.

I feel numb.

I feel empty.

I should be feeling something, anything. Sorrow, depression, sadness, *anything*. But I can't feel, and I don't know how to.

I lay there on the crumpled car as medics fuss over me. I should do something about this situation. I should teleport somewhere, but I don't have the strength, physically and mentally to deal with an exercise requiring every part of me.

"Vee, can you hear me?" I call out to her, in a desperate attempt to communicate. I know it's futile. She's dead. The

woman I vowed to protect, the woman I had saved from death at the hands of her husband, has been taken away. Away by someone even more sadistic and psychotic.

I will make Abigail pay for what she has done.

I will enjoy holding her life in my hands as I slowly torture her for the rest of her days.

And when I'm done with her, I will kill her.

For Vee.

AUTHOR'S NOTE

Thank you for taking the time to read my novella and I hope you liked it.

First I should say sorry for the cliff hanger, don't worry though, I will be extending this into a full novel and I have a plan to make it into a trilogy and possibly two prequel novellas.

I have many WIP's at the moment but the next story I have planned for release, hopefully in the next few months is my Magic and Flames series, with the first book being Rising Inferno which is about a phoenix/witch hybrid.

I also want to give a special thanks to some wonderful people in my life who have pushed me to pursue my dreams and told me time and time and time again that I could do this, that I was good enough to get into the writing game. So thank you first off to my wonderful in real life friends Sam Honna, Emma Bettson, Lani Macdonald and Anna Ivanise-

AUTHOR'S NOTE

vic, who were the first people I told and who have given me their endless support.

I would like to thank my beautiful Critique Partners, Kendra Moreno, Katie Wyatt, Nicole Sanchez and Tamra Shaughnessy for all your support, for putting up with me whenever I'd get all emotional and whine about how I couldn't do it anymore.

Next, a big thank you to authors Skye Mackinnon, Laura Greenwood, Arizona Tape, Tansey Morgan, Yumoyori Wilson and my wonderful Questionable Conversations and Donner crew. All of you are. . . .There are no words to express how much you all mean to me and how much you have helped me through the writing process from your encouragement, support and advice. I would be so lost without you all.

I would like to thank my wonderful editors, Brittany VanLanen of TBR Editing and Eveis Kenevis for making my novella what it was to what it is now. The hours of editing spent because I'm horrible with it HAHA.

Lastly, I would love to thank Brittany VanLanen for designing an amazing cover. It's so amazing and I'll be forever grateful for the time you spent on it.

Oh and of course, thank you to all of you that read my story xx

ABOUT THE AUTHOR

Amara Kent is a true blue Australian, she's an avid reader with a wild imagination. She has always wanted to write but never thought that she would be good enough until some very special people pushed her to pursue writing. She is a lover of horror, the supernatural and dark stories and is a big fan of Stephen King, horror movies, as well as the TV show Supernatural.

Amara is a writer of Dark Urban Fantasy/Paranormal Romance with a splash of horror – she can't seem to NOT put horror elements in her writing.

If you would like to know more about Amara and be kept up to date with future releases and to discuss her books you can follow her at the following:

Amara Kent Facebook Page:
https://www.facebook.com/amara.kent.35

Amara Kent's Facebook Group - Amara's House of Myth and Magic:

https://www.facebook.com/groups/amarashouseofmythandmagic/

Twitter:
https://twitter.com/AmaraKentAuthor

Bookbub:
https://www.bookbub.com/authors/amara-kent

Amazon:
www.amazon.com/AmaraKent/e/B077Z32ZXQ/ref

Made in the USA
Middletown, DE
16 January 2018